MW01248738

PRAISE FOR HAZARDS OF NATURE:

"Like his peers Ron Rash, Claire Davis, Annie Proulx, and Wiley Cash, Brandon Dudley is in the business of carving lives worth living from the hardscrabble topographies of the heart. These are stories that swing between the tough and the tender, stories of regular people trying to find their way in a world filled with heartbreak, and they are not to be missed."

— Christian Kiefer, author of *Phantoms*

"Like the eyes of predators shining from the darkness of the woods, the stories in *Hazards of Nature* burn with a menace that must be feared and confronted. From the tension between father and son, husband and wife, or the tension of mortality itself, spring biting indictments of human frailty and stunning revelation. Powerfully written with empathy and imagination, brutal and beautiful, this chapbook announces Brandon Dudley as a potent new voice in American letters."

— Alan Heathcock, author of *VOLT* and *40*

"Brandon Dudley's stories are hardscrabble mud tracks ripped into the banks of stagnant ponds and the fears that sensitive boys hold onto tightly and don't dare whisper out loud. Every sentence is coiled tightly and strikes just at the moment the reader realizes what is moving in the grass. I couldn't stop reading—I was pulled through like a grip on my hand that I could not shake."

— Jodi Angel, author of *You Only Get Letters from Jail*

HAZARDS
of
NATURE

Stories

BRANDON DUDLEY

Maine Chapbook Series

Selected by Sigrid Nunez
Maine Writers & Publishers Alliance
2021

ISBN: 978-1-7356732-1-9

©2021
Published in the United States of America
by the Maine Writers & Publishers Alliance
Portland, Maine

Publication made possible by grants from the Maine Arts
Commission and the Margaret E. Burnham Charitable Trust.

Cover image by Shawn Rice

Book Design & Editing by Pink Eraser Press

For Becky, Sam, and Liam

CONTENTS

INTRODUCTION

A famous rule for writing stories is that the writer must make something happen to the main characters. Another famous rule is that, for a story to be any good, the thing that happens to the characters should be something bad. Only by putting them through some ordeal can the writer reveal what kind of person a character truly is. Of course, a person engaged in a conflict is probably going to be more interesting to read about than one who's coasting through life, and to be interesting is the most important writing rule of all.

As the title of Brandon Dudley's excellent chapbook suggests, bad things happen to the people in his stories. A young boy is teased past bearing by his brutish father and brothers. A man faces an agonizing choice: to give up either the wife he loves or the children he has always wanted but that she refuses to have. An elderly widower finds solace in his attachment to a tree he has planted but is hopeless when it comes to connecting with his fellow human beings.

These are ordinary people, and the trouble that finds them is ordinary too. Whether or not you've ever been old and isolated, or helplessly bullied, or torn between two equally powerful desires, the range of human emotions here—fear, anger, love, sadness, loneliness, mortification, loss—is sure to be familiar. What makes the stories in *Hazards of Nature* so compelling for me is not just the writer's insightful portraits of his characters' struggles but his sensitivity regarding their pain. And, as someone who believes that humor is an essential element in storytelling and that there is far too little of it in contemporary fiction, I took special delight in his deft use of comedy, most notably in "Animal Sacrifices."

One good test for the quality of a short story is said to be how long the characters continue to exist in your imagination after you turn the last page. The boy Alton of "Coyotes," the old man Harold of "Honey Babe," and, somewhere in the middle of his life's journey, the unnamed narrator of "Animal Sacrifices": each remains as real to me as people I might have actually met. The reason for this is no mystery. Nothing brings a character more vibrantly to life—nothing makes you care more about what happens to them, bad or good—than the compassion of their creator. This is the highest achievement of Brandon Dudley's *Hazards of Nature*.

— *Sigrid Nunez*

HAZARDS
of
NATURE

COYOTES

Alton knew his daddy thought him weak. No matter how hard he willed them not to, his legs trembled when he climbed the ladder to hang tobacco in the barn rafters. He lost his breakfast the time he watched his daddy cut a thin, sharp line down a hog's throat, the thick blood splashing onto the ground and splattering up onto his pants. His brothers, Ronnie and Daniel, tormented him with dead snakes under his blanket and Daddy never bothered to stop them, though as teenagers the pair should have been beyond taunting a nine-year-old.

The time they locked him in the hot, dark shed at the edge of the yard, Alton could hear Daddy's boots on the hard ground outside. He stopped at the locked door.

"Stop crying, boy," he said. "You're too old for this."

"Let me out."

"When you stop crying."

Alton tried. He heard his daddy's footsteps move away, leaving him there to bang on the door in the dark.

* * *

That same summer, just after dark, Alton's daddy came in from locking up the chickens and said he heard coyotes yipping around the barn. "Prolly trying to get at the rabbits."

They heard coyotes often and, when the corn and tobacco were low enough, they could sometimes see them at dusk lurking around the tree line. The past few days, Daddy had seen tracks around the door of the barn and scratches where they'd tried to dig their way in through the rock-hard dirt.

"We gotta go take care of 'em," he said.

Alton stood in the doorway of the kitchen, twisting the dish towel around his hand. The three would go hunt the coyotes and leave him here to clean up supper, he knew, and his pulse quickened at the thought of being left in the empty house alone again. Creatures' faces always hovered just out of sight in the dark windows, their steps creaking on the porch. He would lock the door and turn on all the lights after his daddy and brothers left, but he'd force himself to look out the windows to watch for them so they wouldn't come back to a locked door and know he'd been scared.

"Alton, I mean you."

He felt a surge of relief realizing he wouldn't be left here alone, but it vanished as he noticed his brothers had not moved from the table. "Why ain't they going, too?" He waved the dishrag at Ronnie and Daniel, who turned to their father for his reaction. Alton looked at the floor as his father walked toward him, waiting for the sting of a palm for this backtalk. But instead, he felt Daddy's hand clasp the back of his neck and pull him toward the door. "It's your turn, boy," he said, grabbing the shotgun from the rack on the wall on the way out.

* * *

A dirt road cut along the edge of their property and about 300 yards from the house it turned hard left, like the peak of a triangle. At the far end, in the center of the wide field, was the barn. The road split the farm and divided the crops—corn on one side, tobacco on the other. The tobacco had been cut at the end of the summer and now hung curing in the barn. In another week or so, they would spend long days harvesting the corn, but it was fall and much cooler, so the work was still hard but at least bearable.

Daddy had the shotgun broken open over his arm and Alton carried the lantern. The moon was bright enough that they hadn't bothered to light it. The tall corn they walked next to was washed silver from the moonlight. *Like the ghosts of plants,* Alton thought. The lantern bale screeched in his hand with each step, and he shivered as he peered down the dark rows.

They stopped on top of a small rise. The barn lay in front of them.

"I don't hear nothing," Alton said.

"Probably heard us coming." Daddy snapped the shotgun closed and motioned toward the squeaking lantern. "Hold that quiet."

They slowed as they neared the barn. "See anything?" Daddy said.

"No." In truth, Alton had drawn so close behind his daddy he could barely see past him, but he could feel eyes in the darkness watching them.

When they got to the barn doors, Daddy finally lit the lantern. The orange light and dark hollows of his face made Alton think of a carved pumpkin, rotting and caving in on itself. The warming lantern felt good near Alton's hands, which had already grown stiff from the surprisingly cold night.

He pulled open one of the wide doors as Daddy held the lantern high. Alton scanned past the halo of light for pale orbs blinking in the darkness and braced himself for swift gray blurs pouncing.

Daddy handed Alton the lantern, held a finger to his lips, and pushed Alton into the barn, then gently pulled the doors closed behind them. The light from the lantern was a small raft in the flood of darkness. The moonlight punched through the holes and gaps in the warped and weathered walls, like the night sky had closed in around them, like they were walking through a field of stars.

In the middle of the barn, off to the side, were the rabbit hutches. They had fifteen to twenty at any time, sometimes far more, ready for butchering throughout the year. Good insurance against bad hunting. "You all'd eat clear through the table if I didn't put those rabbits in front of you," Daddy said whenever they tucked into bowls of rabbit stew or ripped into chunks of the peppered meat, fried tough.

Alton hated the butchering days. It wasn't the iron tang of the blood, or the way the mouths ticked open and closed on the severed heads, or even the way his brothers dropped the loops of intestines down the back of his shirt. All that had grown tolerable. It was the sound of the rabbits screeching he hated, screaming like terrified children as Daddy carried them by the scruff of their necks to the chopping block. The barn filled with screams and afterward he heard them for days, like his body collected the sound and echoed it back.

As they got closer to the hutches, they could see a dark mass in front of the far hutch. At the edge of the light a dead rabbit was splayed wide, its stomach blooming like a red flower. The blood had spread in thin rivulets, clotted with gray dust like mud-caked worms.

Daddy crouched and folded the rabbit's leg back until he could see some semblance of the rabbit when it was live and whole. "The runt, that sickly one. They're here all right." Alton expected him to be angry, but an amused smile spread across his face as he looked away into the darkness.

Alton peeked into the hutch. In the back corner, the remaining rabbits huddled. "They're scared," he said. He touched the wooden bars of the hutch and wondered if they could remember what they had seen, if it had made them scared of the dark.

There was a low growl, then scratching at the barn door.

Alton looked to Daddy. "You hear that?"

"I heard."

There was another growl, louder this time, then the yip and howl of a coyote. "They're here," Alton whispered, but Daddy didn't move. The gun still hung loosely at his side.

Something snuffled along the outside wall behind the hutch.

"What do we do?" Alton said.

"We kill them." Daddy smiled at him.

There was a great howl then, long and high. A creature thumped heavily by on the other side of the barn wall.

"You sure those are coyotes?" Alton whispered.

"Course they are. You hear 'em don't you? Come on." Daddy crept to the wall of the barn and peeked through a gap in the warped boards.

"What are we gonna do?" Alton said.

"We're gonna call 'em." Daddy slid the barrel of the shotgun through the gap. "They come around here, then *boom*." He laughed, then breathed deep. He let out a few high-pitched barks that bled into a full-throated howl.

Alton stared at him, wide-eyed. "How'd you learn that?"

"My daddy used to call 'em in some nights. Get 'em in close, take a couple for the pelts, or just for the hell of it. Something to do. I'd teach you if your rattling bones wouldn't scare 'em off." Daddy poked Alton's trembling knee. He turned back to the dark hutches. "I got an idea. Go get that rabbit."

"The dead one?"

"Course the dead one. Go on."

Alton crept into the dark. Back at the front of the barn, there was a *thunk* on the door.

"What was that?" He scrambled to Daddy and pressed against the wall.

"Just get the damn rabbit, Alton. It wasn't nothing." He grabbed Alton's shoulder and pushed him back into the darkness.

Alton trudged off again, this time even slower. He bent low, as if what scared him hung close above his head.

He crouched by the rabbit and poked it, looking for a clean way to pick it up. He noticed the dust surrounding it. "There's no tracks," he said.

"What?"

"There's no coyote tracks. Only our boots."

"Just get on back here."

He picked up the bloody rabbit and held it far in front of him to keep from touching the blue intestines.

Daddy let out a clipped laugh when he saw him. "It's dead," he whispered. "Ain't gonna bite ya."

Alton dropped it in the dirt and squatted over it. "Now what?"

Daddy leaned the shotgun against the wall and turned to Alton. He grabbed the boy's hands and plunged them into the pulpy mess of the rabbit, mashing his fingers down into the guts and pushing his palms into the cooling flesh. Alton yanked away, but Daddy's hard hands were locked around Alton's thin wrists. He yanked again and Daddy let go and Alton sprawled back in the dirt.

Alton's throat tightened and flooded with saliva. His heart flailed in its cage and his lungs hitched in shallow breaths. He wiped his fouled hands on his pants, leaving smears of dark, clotted blood.

"See?" Daddy said. "They're only guts. Nothing to be scared of." He studied Alton a moment and let out a long breath. "You can't grow up so afraid, Alton. You can get scared, but then you gotta force yourself to face it. That's the only way you can get by."

"I ain't scared." Alton's voice cracked.

"You are. And you can't be. A scared man gets taken advantage of. A man like that gets disrespected. And that ain't the kind of men you boys are gonna be."

Alton stared down at his hands. The blood on them had already started to stiffen and dry as he squeezed them into fists.

"I don't have sons like that," Daddy said, pressing his eye again to the gap in the wall. "Maybe your mother would have done it different." His voice was so low Alton barely heard him. He was silent then, staring out at the field, and it was clear he would say no more about that.

"Take the rabbit," Daddy said. He nudged the dead animal with his boot. "Slide him outside."

Rainwater had long pooled on the foundation ledge, rotting the ends of the siding and creating a gap that Alton was able to push the rabbit through. It slopped into the weeds. He tried again to wipe the offal from his hands, but only smeared blood and intestines on his clothes.

Daddy barked and yipped again, then let out an urgent howl. "They'll come now," he said. "You step aside and watch." He slipped the barrel of the shotgun through the gap.

Alton moved a few feet to the side and pressed his eye to a hole. Around the barn, the fields were still washed ghostly by the moon. The corn moved in the breeze like some swaying gray mob surrounding them, pressing closer. He watched the voids between the rows. Then a dark mass rushed in from the right, closing the distance in long strides. The shotgun exploded. Alton threw himself back from the wall, pressing his hands to his ears and crunching his eyes tight.

He felt a hand clamp his wrist and pull, and he saw Daddy speaking, but his voice was watery, swallowed by the blast still echoing in Alton's ears.

"Get up. You're fine," Daddy said, his face flushed with frustration. "Did you see it?"

"It was big." Alton shook his head to clear his buzzing skull.

"Real big. Bigger'n any coyote I've seen." Daddy looked through the gap again. "The rabbit's gone."

Alton felt his stomach loosen and his chest tighten. He didn't dare look out the hole again. "Can't we just set the traps and get home?"

"We ain't here to set traps," Daddy said. He headed toward the doors, and Alton shuffled quickly behind. There, he handed Alton the lantern.

"The doors are stuck," he said.

"What do you mean?"

"They're stuck. I can't open them."

Daddy pushed all his weight against them. The doors bowed

out but didn't open. Through the crack they could see a tobacco stake wedged through the handles outside.

"Who did that? Who did that?" Alton's voice rose.

"Calm down," Daddy said. He pressed his face to the gap between the doors, the shotgun held tight. "This is more than coyotes."

Alton whimpered, a shrill half-cry he couldn't stop until Daddy clamped his fingers onto his cheeks. "Boy, you better knock that off. I said you ain't gonna be that way." Daddy glared at him, his nails pinching into the soft flesh of Alton's cheeks before he finally let go.

To the right, they could still hear panting and quick yips and howls. "The other door," Daddy said.

Alton looked off into the black cavern of the barn. Between them and the door at the far end were the rabbits, then the tractor and the flatbed they pulled behind it. Above them, tobacco dangled like brown fingers. He held the lantern up, the feeble light pooling far too close.

Daddy pulled a tobacco stake from the pile near the door. "Here, take this," he said, handing it to Alton. The wood felt dry and light, and the square point was dull. He felt better, braver, though, with even this rudimentary weapon.

Daddy walked off. He stopped at the edge of the light and turned to Alton. "Come on."

They passed the hutch, Alton careful to step over the small splotch of blood from the dead rabbit. They were next to the tractor when the far door creaked open. The sliver of moonlight grew wide, and in it was the silhouette of a man. Then the door slammed closed, and the man's shape was swallowed by the dark.

"Daddy, Daddy," Alton said. "Who is that?"

"Quiet. Come here." They crouched down by the tractor tire. Daddy motioned for the lantern, and he took it and held it up high. Alton scanned the piles of crates and bales of hay and stacks of tobacco baskets, ready to see some dread face peering out at him.

He looked back to Daddy and realized all the lantern was doing was lighting their exact spot. He shuffled to the edge of the light and held the stake out in front of him like a spear.

"Wait here," Daddy said. Crouching, he moved forward with the light in one hand and the shotgun in the other. At the end of the trailer, he set the lantern on the ground, and peeked around with the shotgun aimed into the darkness.

A moment passed as the two of them waited quiet, listening for movement. Alton could hear shuffling, but over the scramble of his heart he could not pinpoint where it came from.

"I don't see anything," Daddy whispered. He started to move back to Alton.

"The light." Alton pointed to the forgotten lantern.

As Daddy turned, a figure rushed up behind him, a burlap sack hooding its face. It grabbed Daddy, a thick arm wrapping tightly around his neck as it snatched him hollering into the dark.

Alton shrieked and ran from the grunts and screams behind him. He crashed into someone's soft stomach and went sprawling into the dirt. He scrambled away as he felt fingers scrabbling at his ankle. He swung the tobacco stake behind him and felt it connect and heard a cry of pain.

He ran hard toward the light coming from the now-open door. He banged through it into the gray light, then turned and ran deep into the cornfield. He slid into the dirt between the rows of corn and lay flat on the ground with his hands over his head, shaking and trying to hold back the sound of his own crying. He scooted away from the corn, sure his trembling would rattle up through the stalks and give him away. The tobacco stake lay on the ground next to him.

Daddy was dead, he was sure, dragged off and murdered by whoever or whatever had crept into the barn. His mind groped for an escape—sprinting through the field home, crawling slowly on his belly, spending an interminable, cold night hiding until dawn—but every plan ended with him being caught and devoured by the hooded man, dragged off to die the same as Daddy.

Then he heard laughter.

"Alton," he heard. "Come on out."

It was Daddy.

"It was just us!" he said. "There's nothing to be afraid of."

Then it was Ronnie's voice, thick with laughter. "Come on, Alton. We were only fooling with you."

He could hear Daniel, too. The three voices murmured across the field, broken by laughter.

"Aw, hell. Where'd he run off to? Alton!"

"He's prolly back to the house under his bed," Daniel said. "Ran right on the tops a that corn all the way home."

The three of them broke up again, laughing. Alton could imagine Daddy wiping his eyes, the way they watered whenever he had a good, hard laugh.

"Alton!" Daddy's amusement had taken a sharp edge now. "Come on out, boy! There's nothing to be afraid of!"

They were silent, listening for him.

"Little shit knocked the wind out of me," Ronnie said. "Whacked me with something."

"Gave him a tobacco stake," Daddy said.

"Jesus," Daniel said. "Good thing you didn't give him the shotgun."

"You did good, Alton! Now come on!"

Alton could hear them plotting what to do next in low voices, but he couldn't quite make out the words.

"Come on out now, boy! We ain't foolin' no more!" Daddy yelled. But still Alton lay in the dirt, shaking from shame as much as fear. There were no coyotes, he was realizing, only the three of them, his father and brothers. They'd even killed that rabbit, the runt, to scare him.

"He must be back at the house," Daniel said.

"We're going back!" Daddy yelled. "Last chance to come on out, otherwise you're on your own."

Alton still did not stand. He would not go to them. Maybe he would sneak into the house later after they'd fallen asleep. Then he wouldn't have to see them. He rubbed his arms to warm them, the cool ground pulling the warmth from his body, and knew he wouldn't be able to wait long.

He heard Daddy's voice lower. "Get rid of that rabbit and let's go. He'll follow."

The barn door slammed shut, then Daniel grunted as he flung the dead rabbit into the field. The body slapped through the corn and thudded somewhere behind Alton. He shrunk back further as their boots crunched along the road and he lay listening as their voices and laughter faded. It was a long time before he stood and walked out of the field. Far ahead of him, Ronnie had the lantern now and its light swung between them. They rounded the bend toward the house and Alton watched the light shine above the corn. Then it stopped and went out.

They waited around the bend, ready to jump out and scare him. Alton was sure of it. But he wouldn't let them scare him again. He looked at the cornfield, tried to judge what line would lead him back to the house. Then he marched in.

He wasn't supposed to walk through the corn. Daddy had threatened them many times, but Alton didn't care anymore. He would walk out of the dark field, head high and unafraid. Show them something, at least. Once in a while, as he walked, he swung the tobacco stake like a sword, cleaving an ear of corn or two, snapping a few stalks straight through.

Had to be halfway by now, he thought, craning to see above the too tall corn. He planted the stake in the ground and jumped, but still couldn't see. He tried again. His breath clouded the air around him.

He was leaning against the stake, bracing for another jump, when the corn rustled behind him. He turned, but saw nothing but stalks swaying in the breeze. He turned back to the house again, ready to jump, when he heard the first howl.

He wheeled around, the stake in front of him. It was only Daddy, he thought. Trying to scare him again. He let the stake sink in the ground.

But Daddy wasn't behind him, he was hiding on the road around the bend, or already given up waiting and gone back to the house. Alton yanked up the stake and looked into the dark. He took a step back and the corn leaves scraped his neck.

The gaps between the rows were black and deep. Again, he heard the high howl of a coyote. Closer? Where the rows disappeared into black points, shapes twisted in the dark.

A coyote barked.

Alton ran and crashed through the corn, the leaves tearing at his skin. He could hear it, he was sure, the coyote snaking its way through the field after him, the corn rustling and the paws kicking up the soft dirt behind him. He could smell its dank fur and rancid breath full of rotting meat.

His legs pumped harder. The tilled earth, damp from the afternoon rain, was soft under his feet. A rut swallowed his foot and sent him sprawling through the corn. He jumped up flailing the tobacco stake, the stalks snapping around him with each swing.

Alton tried to yell, to roar as loud as he could, but his throat was dry, and it came out strangled and weak and he didn't know which way to face. It could be anywhere. He swung the stake again and again until the corn stalks lay broken in a broad swath around him. His tongue felt thick, and pain jabbed his side with each quick breath.

He straightened, tried to make himself look bigger as he sucked in air and kept watch on the darkness where he'd heard the howls.

"Get out of here! Go!" His voice was weak. He swung the stake toward the darkness between the rows, smacking the ground, the wood stinging the bones of his palm. He shook his hand, trying to knock loose the pain. He felt the rabbit blood then, still sticky on his fingers, the gore still coating his hands and clothes, its scent wafting through the corn.

Somewhere in the dark he heard a sharp bark, then a long, high howl. The night seemed to quiet, but then the lone coyote was echoed by a chorus of howls. Alton knew how they would respond—their ears perked and their sharp snouts sniffing the air before they burst forward to answer the call. They would flank him, close in on all sides, each animal a tooth in a jaw ready to snap shut.

He turned, expecting to see one creeping up behind him. He pivoted and swung again, this time to the right. He turned and swung and turned and swung until his arms burned.

His legs weakened and he had to plant the stake to steady himself when he realized what he'd done. He'd spun and swung and fought, and now had no idea which way to find home.

His breath came in ragged hitches as he circled, looking for the coyotes in the darkness, looking for home through the cornfield. Was the house in front or behind? He could see the moon but couldn't remember if it was of any use for navigation.

He swung the stake again, snapping stalks of corn and stepping toward the darkness. If he pretended that he wasn't scared, if he acted strong enough, the answer would come.

A chorus of howls rose behind him, the sound echoing from everywhere. He imagined the coyotes arced like a scythe across the field, rushing toward him.

A long trail of broken and bent cornstalks unspooled in front of him. An erratic path ripped through the corn, the sharp dark divots of his footprints in the soft dirt, the trail ending in the broken circle around him. Those tracks, that path, that was where he came from. The house was behind him.

Alton spun again; eyes closed as he swung the stake wide. His palms were slicked by sweat and the stake flew off into the darkness. He turned and ran, the stalks snapping around him like gnashing teeth.

He sprinted and waited for the bite at his heel that would pull him down, the writhing, fur-covered mass that would bury him. He imagined his father standing over his dead, mangled body, shaking his head. Alton ran and prayed not to die, until his lungs and muscles burned and suddenly the corn was gone, vanishing from either side of him.

The loose field turned to solid dirt and grass carpeted the soft slope of the backyard. The windows of the house glowed like yellow eyes, watching him as he ran to the shed and jumped inside, slamming the door behind him.

He panted, his back pressed against the door, the rough wood scraping through his shirt with each breath. Inside the shed was quiet but for the filling of his lungs and his pulse flooding his ears.

The sound of coyotes crashing into the door never came. He waited, listening for them snuffling or pacing around the perimeter of the shed, but he heard nothing.

Alton cracked the door until he could see the cornfield. It had grown still, the only evidence of anything wrong were the skewed stalks at the edge of the yard. He closed the door and leaned his head against the wood. He wiped his eyes. Nothing was out there.

"Alton!" he heard. "Alton!" He peeked from his hiding spot and saw Daddy, Ronnie, and Daniel on the dark porch. Far off in the field, a coyote called. "Goddamn it," Daddy said. "Let's go."

Their lanterns creaked as they stomped off across the yard. The far-off shouts grew clearer.

Alton crept out into the dark. Along the road to the barn, three lanterns broke through the night. He watched the lights and listened to Daddy and his brothers shout his name as they marched toward the barn, the three spread along the road like a short string of lights.

Alton walked up to the house. His legs felt shaky and unfamiliar, like they belonged to someone else. He sat on the porch, resting in the small square of light pooled under the kitchen window. He shivered as his sweaty body cooled quickly in the night air.

Down the road, the shouts continued.

Past the barn, a lone coyote howled. The coyote sounded again, and this time, it was answered by a choir, high, sharp barks crashing into and over each other. The lanterns stopped and clustered together, and Alton could see the three of them staring off across the field. They started down the road again, faster now, the lights bouncing in jagged arcs. Daddy's voice grew louder, even though the lights grew more distant. There was a strange urgency to his voice Alton hadn't heard before, but he recognized the fear fraying the edges and smiled. In a few moments, the three would reach the bend, the only spot where they could see both the barn and the house. The coyotes' cries echoed across the field.

As his daddy and brothers reached the bend in the road, Alton moved out of the light. They paused to look back at the house, then disappeared around the corn.

Letting the door hang open, Alton went inside. He imagined his daddy and his brothers and their lanterns wheeling around the barn, their panicked darts into the corn as they searched for his tracks, their shouts and the coyotes' howls growing louder. He turned out the light and sat at the kitchen table, knowing full well there wasn't anything out there to be afraid of.

ANIMAL SACRIFICES

For a long time, when someone would ask if my wife and I had children, I would tell them we'd gotten chickens instead, and that was enough. They'd look at me like I was making some stupid joke, but I wasn't. Not really. We'd had chickens once, for a little while, but something had killed them all. And if I couldn't even keep them alive, what good would I have been to a child?

The morning Steph and I found the first dead chicken, its gray feathers sprayed across the far edge of the yard like patchy frost, was almost a year after she'd told me she'd changed her mind about having children. Before we'd gotten married, we'd talked of it often. Even settled on tentative names. Julia, after her grandmother. Shawn, after my father. But after all these years together, what I thought were good, happy years, she didn't want to have children anymore. She didn't want Julia or Shawn. But I still did.

Outside, the breeze tumbled the feathers across the lawn. "Goddammit," I said, standing at the kitchen window. Steph's face reflected in the glass as she rested her chin on my shoulder. Her eyes widened. "Oh, no," she said.

"I'll take care of it," I said.

Out in the yard, I stood over the feathers. Some of them had blown back toward the run and caught in the chicken wire. There was no blood, but one clump seemed to be held together by a chunk of flesh. The edge of a wing, it looked like.

The chickens were different colors, brown and tan and gray and black and white and red, a flock of random breeds brought home in a cardboard box from Tractor Supply, along with an assortment of feeders and waterers and a heat lamp. As they grew, we gave the girls old lady names: Eleanor, Ruth, Doris, Harriet, Henrietta, and the now-dead gray one, Myrtle. I always liked the little white one, Eleanor, because she was so much smaller and always running frantically after the others. If I could have picked one to be eaten, it would have been the big brown one, Ruth, who pecked my legs so much I'd taken to wearing big rubber boots around the yard.

I opened the door to the coop, an old playhouse I'd converted earlier that summer. The chickens clustered on their roost, shifting in the light. Eleanor huddled in a corner. Ruth didn't even try to come peck at me.

Behind them, old, flowered wallpaper peeled from the plywood walls. Steph wanted to build something new, but I told her I could make this work. She'd pointed at the old paint on the trim, the way it cracked in misshapen rectangles, the ridges underneath the flakes; all tell-tale signs of lead paint. "They're going to get lead in their systems. Then so will we," she said, putting a hand to her belly. I wanted to ask, *Why does it matter?* But instead, I said, "Chickens aren't stupid enough to eat lead paint." But for all I knew, they probably were.

"Why can't we just buy one already made?"

"I don't need to." I closed the door to the playhouse, some flecks of paint fluttering to the ground. "I'll take care of this. I'll show you. It'll be better. Cheaper."

I didn't want to tear it down, I guess, because I wanted to remind her of what we could still have. Maybe she'd see the chickens out there in this old playhouse and some desire would start to grow, some need for something more. It was a stupid and desperate plan, but at the time that's exactly what I was.

So I'd gone about painting over the poisonous trim and stapling hardware cloth over the wide, rotten window. I wrestled the bottom of the fence into a clumsy L-shape before burying it a couple feet under the ground because I'd read online that was the best way to keep animals from digging their way inside. I'd topped the run with loose bird netting instead of chicken wire, tired of slicing my hands on the sharp fencing. In the end, it looked like some cross between a playhouse and a hillbilly prison, but I was sure I'd built it secure enough.

As I walked around the coop that morning, I could see in the loose dirt at the base of the fence what looked like tracks from a small dog. A fox. It had to be. But there were no tracks inside the run, no obvious signs of entry. I walked back over to the feathers. "How'd he get you?"

Steph walked up behind me, her brightly patterned pajama pants dulled in the morning light. She held her arms tight against her chest. "Oh, poor Dorothy." She walked around, looking at the feathers, frowning.

"That was Myrtle. We don't even have a Dorothy."

"Oh. What killed her?"

"Fox." I pointed to the tracks. "I think."

"Well, I'm sorry, babe," Steph said. "I was worried that netting wasn't enough."

"A fox couldn't get through that."

"Tell that to Myrtle."

* * *

When we'd gotten the chickens that spring, they were nothing more than little balls of fluff. We'd watched them grow bigger, joking about their awkward teenage years as they'd sprouted motley feathers. All summer and into the fall they'd wandered about the yard pecking at the grass, eating all the bugs and ticks.

We'd bought the house six years before, not long after we'd gotten married. Back then, a playhouse in the backyard, even an old rotten one, had meant something. It was a goal, not some eyesore to work around. Maybe someday I'd fix it up for kids, then build a swing set and a sandbox nearby.

The house stood on a good lot, woods on two sides, neighbors packed in across the street and next door, but still plenty of places for kids to play undisturbed. At least that was what we thought before. It was what I still thought.

The night Steph told me she'd changed her mind, she squeezed my hand and said she still loved me.

"But you don't want to have a baby with me," I said.

"I love you, and I love what we have, and I'm not ready to change that."

"So, you might be ready someday?"

She let go of my hand. "No. I'm sorry. I shouldn't have said it that way."

"You should haven't said you wanted kids to begin with, if you were just going to change your mind."

"I didn't know I was going to change my mind! I didn't know how things were going to turn out."

"Turn out? What did I do wrong?"

"Please stop twisting my words around."

"I'm not the problem here."

I'd stormed out of the house and slammed the door so hard I broke the frame around the latch. I fixed it the next day, but you can still see where the crack is, if you know where to look.

* * *

We settled into a delicate truce, every conversation a fragile barrier between us and all the things we'd left unsaid. I could feel her tense up every time a movie character had a baby, or when commercials showed a family frolicking in a park or some other cheesy scene. Sometimes I couldn't take it, and I'd turn the TV off, or I'd pretend to go to the bathroom, or I'd go to the kitchen to make another drink. But things settled down, eventually, or maybe we just grew numb to the tension of it all.

Eventually, there were whole days when I didn't think about kids. But then we got the chickens and I put them in the old playhouse and thought of children constantly.

I knew very little about chickens before we got them. I still don't know much, I guess. I would joke that ours were freeloaders, that our first eggs would cost hundreds of dollars in supplies and feed and coop construction. Eighteen eggs at the grocery store cost $1.89. Less if we caught them on sale.

But I couldn't wait for those first eggs. I dreamed of thick dark yolks the size of golf balls, the whites firm enough to pool on the pan, to hold it all together in a perfect circle.

Neither of us ever had chickens before, or anything beyond the usual dogs and cats. We'd both grown up in the suburbs, in clusters of cul-de-sacs locked together like the teeth of a zipper, the closest thing to a farm the drawings of cows and barns on the milk carton.

How often people do that: take the life they were given at birth and reverse it, declare *This is the way I'll be different.* I had a huge family, and so I don't want children. I was never allowed pets, so now I run a zoo. My parents were tech freaks, so I went back to the land. I grew up in some hippie commune, so I was the first in line to have a computer implanted in my brain. We become farmers or cyborgs, a pendulum swinging slowly back and forth, generation after generation.

I tried to convince myself that without children maybe our lives could be better. We could do all the things kids would have prevented, things I heard friends lament the loss off: travel, the ability to change plans on a whim, sleep in, think coherent thoughts without a child screaming, dump money into silly projects, like keeping chickens, without worrying about depleting college savings. Maybe this was the pendulum swinging toward childless farmer. At least I found some solace in watching the chickens bop across the yard, their feathered butts bouncing as they ran.

Sometimes I harbored fantasies of more animals, like ducks, or goats. We could spend our Saturdays running a booth at the farmer's market in town, selling eggs and chèvre and soap. No worries about fucking up a kid along the way.

But more and more the chickens felt like a way to prove myself, a way to change her mind. If she could just see me taking care of the girls, she would know for sure I could be a good father.

And so I would thrill with hope every time I caught her watching me care for them, feeding them or checking on the coop or shooing them back to safety when a hawk circled lazily around the yard. It was promising, I thought, that she would always ask after the eggs, even though I always had to tell her there were none yet. Maybe soon the mother sleeping in her would wake.

But now Myrtle was dead.

"It's nature," Steph said that night. "Bad things happen."

"I can fix it," I said, looking out at the dark shadow of the coop.

* * *

I dug around in the back of the shed. Underneath the ripped-up tarp we used to drag away leaves and the cheap hose that always kinked, I found it: a rusted trap, a rectangle of thick wire with metal doors at both ends. The old owners had left it behind, along with some broken rakes and an ungodly number of paint cans. I'd pressed them at the closing to come pick up their shit, and they'd promised, but I'd failed to get anything in writing, and I eventually gave up calling their agent. Now all this garbage was still stacked in the back of the shed, taking up the space for the potting bench Steph wanted but I still hadn't built. Every spring I said I'd get rid of all the junk, but I never had. I would do it soon. It could be a surprise for her someday.

I pulled the trap out and set it on the grass. I knelt next to it and pulled up the doors, flipped the thin levers on the side, fiddled with the metal plate in the center. In a few minutes, I'd figured out how to set it, and I could feel the tension on the levers holding the doors open. I stuck a finger through the wire, pressed the metal plate, and the doors slammed shut.

* * *

The next morning, the trap was empty. I'd set it next to the coop and baited it with a can of cat food, but it sat undisturbed, the brown goop hardened over and covered in slugs.

The morning after, though, the doors had been tripped, blocking the view of whatever waited inside. I stepped quietly across the yard to see what I'd captured, waiting to see the creature that had been killing my chickens. But the trap was still empty, and so was the can of cat food. I kicked the trap, and the chickens inside the coop squawked. Steph watched from the kitchen window.

"Should you be putting the trap right next to the chickens?" she said when I went back inside. "Won't the bait draw animals right where we don't want them?"

"It's fine," I said, but later that day, when I re-baited the trap with some old fish I found in the freezer, I moved it to the edge of the yard and wedged it under a bush.

The trap sat there undisturbed for a few days, and Steph often looked out at it skeptically. Then one morning the doors were down again. This time, I knew something was inside the moment I stepped into the backyard. The metal rattled as the animal inside moved around, calling and crying.

"I got it!" I called back into the house. Steph was upstairs, getting ready for work. I grew more excited as I walked across the yard. I'd only ever seen a fox as a copper blur darting across my headlights at night.

But when I could see past the bush and inside the trap, I was surprised to find a black mask on a pile of gray fur. The raccoon slunk back and bared its teeth. I crouched down to get a closer look.

"Oh my gosh," Steph said. "He's so cute."

I hadn't heard her come up behind me and I jumped. "Look! I caught it," I said, smiling.

"That ate the chicken?" she said. Her lips pursed and she crossed her arms.

"Myrtle. And yeah, they eat chickens."

Steph shrugged. "I don't know."

I pulled my phone out and looked it up. "Yeah, see, they do."

"He looks really young." She took a step closer, and the raccoon edged forward, reaching its paws through the bars. Steph laughed and stuck a finger toward it.

"Don't!" I slapped her hand.

"Ow!" Steph pulled her hand to her chest. "Goddamn. Why'd you do that?"

I turned my phone toward her. "They can have rabies. And they'll rip a chicken apart. It says so. Says they can rip them right through a fence."

"I am not a chicken," Steph said, each word slow and deliberate. "And that thing clearly doesn't have rabies."

"I didn't want you to get hurt."

"So you slapped me?" She stood and walked back toward the house. "Let him go. He's not going to hurt anything. Christ."

"If I let him go, he's just going to come back."

She stopped and turned around. "Because you fed him cat food. He's practically a baby. Take him somewhere and let him go."

* * *

I drove the raccoon down to the boat launch a few miles from our house. It was mid-week and late in the season, and all the pleasure boats were gone. The few trucks parked in the lot likely belonged to fishermen.

Through the window of the back of my SUV, I could see the trap covered by an old blanket. The raccoon had yowled and thrashed as I drove, but quieted when I parked. I put on a pair of cheap orange gardening gloves and opened the hatch. A stink of piss rolled out of the car, and I regretted leaving the tarp back in our garage. The raccoon hissed, blinking in the light when I pulled off the blanket. I reached to pick up the trap and the raccoon lunged, and I jumped back.

"You little fucker."

I whacked the side of the cage, and the raccoon went wild, lurching and slamming into the sides. When it calmed, we stared at each other, both hearts pounding.

The sound of a motor broke the standoff. A small skiff slid toward the dock with a man sitting at the rear, a little boy in the bow. They both had dark hair, the same olive skin.

"Shit." The last thing I wanted was an audience for my stupid fight with a baby raccoon.

The boy waved and I instinctively waved back before realizing I was still wearing the orange gardening gloves. I pulled them off and set them in the back of the car.

The man tied off his boat and climbed up the short ladder to the dock, the boy in front of him. His truck must have been parked behind me because they headed my way.

"Whatcha catch there?" he said, peering in the back of the SUV. He whistled when he saw the raccoon. "Look, Bobby," he said to the boy.

"I think he killed one of my chickens."

"You going to kill him?" the boy asked, leaning forward to look at the raccoon.

I blinked down at him. He was younger than I thought at first, maybe five or six. "I was going to let him go."

He looked up at me then to his father, who shrugged, then he looked back to the raccoon pacing in the trap.

The man looked out to the water. "If you live nearby, he'll make his way back, eventually. Nice easy buffet like that, they don't forget. If it were him, anyway."

"You don't think it was?"

"Seems a bit young. Could have, sure. But this age, they don't tend to be that resourceful, unless your coop wasn't very secure."

I felt my face flush. "It was."

"We don't exactly got a raccoon shortage around here," the

man said. "Plus, these little bastards carry rabies."

"Dad."

"What? Is bastard a bad word?"

"That's what mom says."

The man rubbed the back of his finger against the outside of the cage, and the raccoon drew closer before the man put his hand back in his pocket. "If I were you, I'd let him go for a little submarine ride," he said. The little boy laughed. "But it's your raccoon," the man said as they turned and headed to their truck.

I stood watching as the man backed the truck down into the boat ramp, the boy on his lap helping steer. The man turned the trailer around like it was second nature. He talked to the boy the whole way, teaching him how to steer it right into place. When I had borrowed our neighbor's trailer to clear out some brush, it had taken me twenty minutes to get it backed up between the garage and the trees bordering our property. Even then, I'd still never gotten it quite where I'd wanted it, and Steph and I had to lug the brush halfway across the yard.

The man went about his business a little slower than he really needed to, taking his time loading up his fishing poles and ratcheting up the boat. He looked over and I turned away, grabbing the trap and yanking it out of the car. It was awkward to carry, and I held it far from my side as I took it down to the water. Over at the dock, the man nodded at me over the bed of his pickup truck. The boy rested his chin on the open passenger window and watched. I walked further down the bank. I could still see the boat and the man, but the little boy at least was out of sight.

The raccoon jumped back and forth, the trap tilting wildly as I held it over the water, hesitating. Maybe this little raccoon really was nothing more than a harmless baby. Maybe he was completely incapable of hurting our chickens. But what if he could? What if he had killed Myrtle after all? What if I let him go and he came back and killed the rest of the girls? What would Steph think then?

I heard the truck roar to life, the deep throaty bass of the engine, and before I could doubt myself again, I dropped the cage. It slapped into the river and the water roiled as it pulled the raccoon under. Bubbles broke the surface as the gray mass, barely visible in the murk, thrashed in the cage. It careened from one side to the other, frantic, then gradually slowed.

Finally, the raccoon was still.

The man honked his horn as he drove off, the small skiff dripping a long trail of water up and out of the boat launch.

After some time, I pulled the trap out of the water, and the raccoon lay in a pile like some sodden stuffed animal. I opened the trap and let it slide into the water, where it sank next to the shoreline, its body gently rocked under the surface by the slow waves.

* * *

When Steph got home, I was scrubbing the raccoon piss out of the back of my car.

"How did it go?"

"He won't bother the girls anymore."

"What do you mean?"

I told her. About the man and the little boy, and what he'd said. About the raccoon and the water, though I told her it had been quick. She looked at me, horrified. "How could you do that? What the hell were you thinking?"

"He was going to kill our chickens."

"You don't even know if it had done anything. It was just a little baby."

I tried to convince her I was right. That it was tough but necessary. That I'd stepped up and done what I'd needed to do. But she looked disgusted and didn't speak to me again that day.

She was probably right. I should have let it go. It might have lived a long, happy life by the water.

* * *

A few days later, I found more feathers in the yard.

This time, two chickens were dead: Ruth, and the red one, Doris. There were tracks again around the coop, but no signs of digging. The bird netting topping the enclosure lay undisturbed, tied and stapled all around. Surely if something had gotten in that way it would have torn the thin netting, likely gotten so entangled it would still be hanging there.

Steph stood in the light of the kitchen window, sipping her coffee, watching.

Since the raccoon, I felt like she was always watching me, staring while I cooked dinner, or read, or as I watched TV. Like she was evaluating her life with me and left wanting.

* * *

Weeks passed. I had replaced the bird netting and secured the top of the run with chicken wire, even covered a few small holes in the plywood with hardware cloth—holes nothing larger than a mouse could have wriggled through, but I covered them anyway.

Then one night, as we lay in bed watching a movie on the laptop, we heard someone yelling out in the yard. "HEY! HEY!" The yells sounded hoarse, like some crazed smoker screaming in our yard.

"Who the fuck is that?" I said.

Steph jerked awake. She lay on the far side of the bed, and I'd not realized she'd fallen asleep. "What?"

"Someone's out there."

"HEY! HEY!"

"What do they want?" Steph said.

"I don't know." My throat felt full, choking off my words. I got out of bed and looked out the window, but the backyard was dark. I wished I'd stashed a baseball bat or something under the bed, but I had nothing.

I looked over at Steph, sitting up in bed bathed in the blue light of the laptop, her phone in her hand. "Be careful," she called after me as I went downstairs.

I could see nothing from the backdoor, but the yelling sounded closer now, not far from the deck. I flicked on the floodlight.

Caught in the light, standing in the middle of the yard, was a fox.

"Hey! Hey!" it cried.

"What the fuck?" I couldn't mesh the two: the sound and the creature, the almost-human voice coming from the fox. My heart was still pounding, and I felt stupid, then angry. "It's the fucking fox!" I yelled. The bedroom window upstairs creaked open.

The fox froze in the yard when I yelled, and it stayed frozen as I stepped out onto the deck. "Get out of here! Go on!" I slammed the door behind me, but the fox didn't move.

I stepped off the deck, out into the yard, but the fox stood rooted in its spot.

"Hey!" the fox cried again.

"Go!" I yelled. I stepped farther into the yard, closer now to the fox, but it still wouldn't leave, its eyes glowing silver and empty at the edge of the light.

I walked within twenty, maybe fifteen feet of the fox. I knew if I looked back at the house, I'd see Steph's silhouette in the window, but I didn't want to turn away from the fox. Each step took a little more effort—my feet grew heavier and the air around me felt colder. Finally, the fox moved toward me. I stepped back. "Go on! Go!"

I looked around for a stick, anything, but saw nothing. I stepped back again, keeping my eyes on the fox until I made it back to the deck. I stumbled a bit, misjudging the top step, as I backed toward the grill and grabbed the rusted grill brush. The fox seemed closer now.

"Get out of here!" I waved the grill brush and stepped toward him, down the steps.

I kept walking closer, brandishing the grill brush, but the fox still wouldn't move. "Go on!" He still didn't move. "Get out of here, you fucking asshole!" I hurled the brush and it hit the ground and bounced past the fox, who jumped to the left a little but still did not leave.

The fox moved, finally, to go smell the grill brush, then trotted off toward the woods, where it disappeared.

I turned to see Steph in the doorway.

"That's so strange," she said. "He wasn't scared at all. And I had no idea they sounded that way."

I was suddenly aware of how hard I was breathing. "I scared it off."

"I think you just hurt its feelings. Not every day a fox gets called a fucking asshole." She laughed as she went inside, leaving me alone in the yard.

* * *

I worked as a writer and copyeditor for a local news circular, a shitty little one full of local business news and cheap advertising. The next day in the office I got dirty looks from Larry, my editor and the only other full-time employee, as I searched for videos of fox cries on YouTube. I tried to explain, but he frowned and went back to his editing.

"Knock it off," he finally said during the fifth video. He picked up proofs of the Around Town section, a mind-numbing list of spaghetti supper fundraisers and yard sales I was supposed to have finished an hour ago.

"That's killing my chickens. It's a gray fox," I said, pointing to the animal frozen on my screen.

"Well, it's obnoxious. So, knock it off and finish these so I can go home." He dropped the proofs back on my desk.

I closed the browser, but I stayed restless and distracted, the calls looping in my head, unable to shake the itch of Steph's eyes on the back of my neck as I crept across the yard toward the fox.

Larry stared at me from his office, so I grabbed the proofs and tried to work.

That afternoon, on my way home, I stopped at the sporting goods store next to Target. It mostly sold golf clubs and running shoes, but in the back corner there were hunting supplies. I walked the aisles, past turkey calls, bottles of deer urine, tubes of camo face paint, and cardboard cubes stuffed with dull arrows, looking for anything that might kill the fox.

As I exited one aisle, I saw a man leaning on the glass counter, the display in front of him full of knives and handguns. Racks of shotguns and rifles leaned against the wall behind him.

"Can I help you?" he said. He had a deep voice and a thick red beard.

"No, I'm just looking," I said, ducking back down an aisle.

I found myself in front of a display of Airsoft guns, toys that shot little plastic pellets. I picked one up, surprised by how realistic it looked. Like AR-15s I had seen on the news.

"That's a fun one." A teenager in a green smock appeared behind me, the store logo on his chest. "Your kid into Airsoft?" he asked. "My friends and I have wars out in the woods."

"No." I set the gun back in the display. "I'm trying to kill a fox."

"Well, that's not gonna do it."

"I know," I said, unable to mask my frustration. "I was just looking."

"If you're looking for a real gun, Bill can help you over at the counter."

"I'm not sure I need one. I was thinking maybe a slingshot or something."

"Shotgun would be easier. But I guess you could try that." The boy motioned toward the rack of slingshots hanging above jars of steel balls and marbles. "Doable, maybe, if you practice." The boy pointed down to the far end of the aisle. "We got some nice pellet guns down there, too. That'd work, as long as you're close enough and get them in the right spot." The boy looked at my tie, down at my dress shoes. "You ever shoot before?"

"Yes." I'd gotten a Red Ryder for Christmas when I was nine. I'd killed a blue jay and felt so bad as I stroked the iridescent feathers that I never shot the gun again.

"Like I said, best bet's a shotgun. A 20 gauge will work, but you can go smaller. A .410 will do, as long as you aren't trying to shoot at any real range. Or a pellet gun, like I said, if that makes you more comfortable." He looked up, a good half foot shorter than me, the faint haze of a mustache above his lip.

"Show me the 20 gauge."

* * *

"Come to bed," Steph said. "If you hear it, you can try to take care of it then."

"No, I'll wait down here." I was sitting on the deck, the shotgun resting across my knees.

"It's cold."

"I've got my coat."

"It's going to smell you."

"Didn't seem to care the other night."

Steph stood behind me, rubbing her arms. "You don't need to do this."

"It'll kill the rest of them if I don't."

"You know what I mean."

I didn't respond.

"They're just chickens. We can always get more."

"They're not *just* chickens, they're *our* chickens. They have names. *We* gave them names."

She turned away. "I'm going to bed. Don't fall asleep and blow your foot off with that stupid thing."

"I'm fine. Go inside. You're too loud."

Steph let the door slam. *Thanks*, I thought. I sighed, my breath forming a dense cloud. She was right, it was cold, and even though the air bit through my thin coat, I couldn't go inside and get anything warmer, not after that.

An hour later, I was still there, bored and freezing, wondering if Steph was still awake. Our bedroom window was dark. The other window, in the room across the hall from our bedroom, was dark, too. We'd originally planned to turn it into a nursery, but it had only accumulated junk. Steph had mentioned something about making it a guest bedroom a few months before, and I had walked out of the room. If we'd had a child, I never would have been sitting in the dark with some stupid gun, never would have wanted to wake up a baby. We never would have even had time for chickens.

I shook my head and pulled out my phone, but it was dead. I'd killed the battery scrolling through Facebook and looking up videos on YouTube about the gun I'd bought. I'd taken a picture of the shotgun laying across my legs, posted it with the caption "Time to take care of the fox killing our chickens."

The first response was from my brother—"Don't shoot your balls off!" and a laughing emoji—so I deleted the post.

It was close to midnight, I guessed. Maybe I would go inside, pretend to go to the bathroom, then peek in and see if Steph was asleep. If she was, I would go sleep on the couch. Or maybe I could sneak into bed without waking her up.

Something rustled in the brush at the edge of the yard. I stood slowly, pulling the shotgun toward my shoulder as I tried to pinpoint the sound.

The fox stepped into the yard from the woods and paused, surveying it like he owned the place.

The sights wobbled as I tried to aim the shotgun, the barrel jumping with each beat of my heart. I steadied it on the fox as my lungs started to burn. I'd been holding my breath, and I sucked in air and blinked and lost track of the fox.

Breathe, I thought. *Squeeze the trigger slowly.* Repeating in my head all the things I'd heard on the YouTube videos.

I found the fox again, steadied the sights. The fox ignored me as it walked across the yard. I glanced up at the dark window of our bedroom, then back at the fox. It loped closer to the chicken coop. I lined up the sights, then breathed out.

I pulled the trigger.

Nothing happened.

I yanked the gun from my shoulder. *What the hell.* Then I saw it, the safety. *God fucking dammit.* I flicked off the safety and looked up for the fox, now trotting around the chicken coop, sniffing at the fence.

I pulled the gun to my shoulder again, swiveled toward the fox, sighted, and fired. Dirt kicked up right behind the fox and it sprinted off into the woods.

The blast echoed through the yard and bounced off the trees. As it faded, I realized how quiet the night had been. A light turned on behind me, Steph's dark shape looming in the window. Next door, the floodlight in the backyard turned on.

* * *

The police cruiser sat in our driveway, the siren blessedly off but the light bar still strobing, bouncing off the houses around us. Most of the windows had gone dark again, but I knew the neighbors were still watching.

The cop was in the middle of writing a series of tickets. One for shooting within town limits. One for endangering people or property. One for violating the noise ordinance. One for hunting out of season.

"I'm not sure I even hit the fox."

"Hunting's hunting, whether you actually hit anything." The cop paused and looked at Steph, who stood there with her arms crossed. "Or not."

"I might have hit it."

"He missed," Steph said.

"I'd say it might be in your interest to apologize to your

neighbors, too." He waved his pen at the mostly dark houses. Across the street, a light shone through a curtain in an upper window, the fabric brightly colored and plastered with some sort of cartoon characters. Puppies, maybe. "Got three calls about this," the officer said. "Real pissed."

"I'm not—" I let out a long breath. "We were going to give them eggs, when we finally had some. I wasn't trying to—"

The officer shrugged. "Your call. You're the one who has to live here. How many chickens you have left?"

"Three. The others got eaten by the fox."

"Could have been a fisher. Rare, but they're around." He must have seen the confusion on my face. "A fisher cat. We used to have chickens when I was a kid. Lost some to fisher cats, never any sign of them. A fox will dig his way in, sometimes jump. A raccoon will bust through chicken wire, kill everything, rip the heads off. Make a big mess. Fisher's like some ghost, gets in and out god knows how. Hardly know it was there."

I looked over at Steph, my mouth open. "What the fuck's a fisher cat?"

The officer looked at Steph like he was sorry for her. "Animal control will be here tomorrow."

"For the fox?" I asked.

"To inspect your coop. You need a permit." The officer handed me the tickets.

The tickets felt thin in my hand, which trembled in the cold. "A permit?"

"Yeah, you were supposed to get one before you got the chickens. It's a $100 fine for each bird. And if your coop's not up to spec, she'll confiscate the birds."

"What the fuck."

The officer scowled at me, annoyed, then looked at Steph. "Have a good night, ma'am."

Steph said thank you and apologized again before she turned to go back inside.

"Don't go shooting anything else, sir," the officer said as he went to his car.

I stood in the driveway, the door to the house slamming behind me, the door to the cruiser slamming in front of me. The officer drove off, his lights still bouncing off the surrounding houses and flashing in the trees.

I didn't go inside. Instead, I walked around the side of the garage, past the back deck to the chicken coop. Inside, three dark shapes huddled together on their roost. The tickets from the cop were in my hand, the night too dark to read the fines.

The house behind me was dark, too. I scanned the tree line, but there was no sign of the fox, only its tracks and the spot where the shotgun pellets had scraped into the dirt.

The fox would be back, I was sure of it. Or the fisher cat, whatever that was. Or maybe the mother of that raccoon. Whatever was out here, killing my chickens. My hundred-dollar fine chickens, plus the tickets, and everything else they cost me.

I saw it then, in the back of the nesting box: a single egg. The chickens watched silently as I picked up the egg, small and pale and surprisingly cold.

All this for one goddamn egg.

I walked back to the house. In the kitchen, I pulled out the frying pan and sprayed it with oil. The fragile shell cracked easily and I fried it then and there and slid it onto a plate.

"What are you doing?" Steph said behind me.

"We finally had an egg." I didn't turn around.

"Why are you doing this?"

I waved the spatula at the backyard. "I might as well get something out of all this. I might as well get one fucking egg. One tiny thing I want."

She stepped toward me, her voice hard and angry. "You need to decide what you really want."

"I know what I want. I want *children*, Steph. I want *them*."

"More than you want me."

"That's not fair."

"It's not. I know that." Her voice softened and she turned and leaned against the wall. "All of this, everything you do, none of it is for me, or even for us. It's for them. It's all just you trying to change my mind. I know that, and I've been waiting, hoping you'd be able to move past it. But I can't live with the constant reminder that being with me, just me, is not enough. And I want you to have enough." She was crying now, though her voice was still calm. "It's not fair to either of us to go on this way. So, you need to decide what you want more." She turned and walked back upstairs.

On my plate, the fried egg had grown cold. I threw it in the trash and went back outside. I sat on the steps of our deck and shivered long into the night, running through every part of our relationship: her eyes the day we first met, the way we used to wake up hungry for each other, how she looked in her wedding dress, waking up on an air mattress our first morning in our new house, the feel of her hand the night she told me things had changed. I tried to find where things had gone wrong, what signs I had missed, or what I might have done differently, but I couldn't figure it out. She had changed in ways I hadn't, and now I had to decide if I loved her enough to change, too. If I loved her enough to let our children go.

I tried to prepare myself for leaving her, tried to piece together the words to tell her I needed more. I imagined the future with some new wife who would have my children in some blank house I couldn't quite see. I tried to imagine the intensity of the start of a relationship with someone new, remembering the way Steph and I couldn't seem to touch each other enough, the way we couldn't be apart. Did that sort of love come twice?

It was easier to imagine the children, to feel what it was like holding their hands, the smell of cake and smoke as they blew out birthday candles, their weight on my lap.

But I couldn't see their faces. I didn't know their names.

I tried to see them, to name them, but I couldn't make them real. Without Steph, there could never be Shawn or Julia. Those children, my children, were lost forever. No matter what I decided that night—whether I stayed with Steph or left to try again—that part of my life was over.

Eventually, late that night, I walked across the yard and opened the door to the chicken coop. The remaining birds were huddled together in the corner of their roost. Henrietta, and Harriet, and little Eleanor. I left them there, the door wide open, offering them to whatever prowled out in the dark.

I went inside and lay in bed next to Steph. Despite everything, she still moved closer to me. I could feel her there in the dark, silently crying—in relief or anger or happiness or more, everything she'd bottled up over the last year. I kissed her and told her what I had decided, which was that I loved her enough, and I was sorry.

And when I finally slept that night, I dreamt of screaming foxes, of dark-eyed raccoons, of ghostly fisher cats. All the creatures I knew and some I didn't, their eyes shining at the dark edges of the yard, creeping closer to the open door of the chicken coop. I dreamt of the chickens huddled together in the dark, scanning the empty windows of the house, waiting for me to rescue them. But I couldn't save them.

When I woke up the next morning, I knew they were gone.

The years since then have been good, and happy. We've traveled and explored and taken risks and grown deeply into each other in ways we never could have with the distraction and pressures of other lives.

But sometimes, when Steph isn't around and people ask about children, I don't mention the chickens at all. *We had children, almost*, I say, and they look at me with pity. It's selfish, forcing them to imagine miscarriages and stillbirths, the horrible losses we must have endured to get to the word *almost*. I know it's wrong, but sometimes I just need someone to look at me and see what I've lost.

And though I try not to, even after all this time I sometimes look out at the spot where the old chicken coop used to be. I wouldn't have made a good farmer, I know that now, but I still wonder what sort of father I might have been. I wonder who my children would have become.

But I'll never know. I loved my wife, I love her still, and because of that love there are some things I can never know.

HONEY BABE

It was the middle of winter when Harold felt the urge to grow something. The snow lay thick over a layer of ice below, a death trap for an old man with fragile bones, so the trip to the hardware store was out of the question. It was unlikely they'd have seed this deep into winter anyway, the garden section likely full of snow blowers and bagged salt.

He was going to let the urge pass, wasn't sure where it came from anyway, when he remembered the heart-sized peach he'd sliced for his morning yogurt. He'd delicately knifed the flesh away from the pit and tossed it in the trash. He dug it out and found it covered in coffee grounds and bits of paper towel that he rinsed off in the sink.

But what to do about soil? The ground was frozen solid, and he wasn't about to become one of those old men found dead in their driveways, frozen to a shovel. In the back of the garage, though, were piles and shelves full of old junk, and he was sure there was a long-dead potted plant stashed there somewhere. He scrounged through it all, moving aside boxes of Christmas decorations he hadn't put up in at least thirty years, boxes of old photo albums, stacks of framed pictures he'd taken down long ago.

Tucked in the back on a low shelf was a dusty old pot, a poinsettia once, he thought. Something the church had dropped off along with an invitation, both of which had eventually withered and died. He stuck the peach pit in the desiccated soil, wondered briefly about nutrients and fertilizer. Did those necessary things decay? Or did they lay dormant, waiting for seed and water and sunlight? He didn't know. But he pressed the pit into the soil and took the pot to the bathroom, where he watered it with the showerhead, the dust and cobwebs slipping from the outside of the pot and swirling down the drain.

* * *

By spring the pit had germinated. A tender shoot curved its way through the soil before growing into a straight, soft green stalk that gradually transformed into something harder and darker, until it was like a thin brown finger pressing its way toward the sky.

Through the early spring Harold checked on it every day, careful to keep the soil just moist enough. He turned the pot a little every afternoon to keep the tree from leaning sharply toward the window. He found himself talking to the little tree, asking it questions about where it thought it was going, or if it had enough water. He wiped the dust from the leaves with a damp cloth, his touch lingering on every thin new leaf, each one a tiny little finger grabbing onto his own.

In the warm days of late April, Harold took the tree outside to his porch for the first time. He set it carefully on the rail to catch the light, then looked at the trees separating his yard from the neighbors. There was no wind, but he pulled a chair up anyway, just in case, and sat near the little tree. As the sun moved across the porch, the pair shifted to follow it. And that was how he spent his days, chasing the rays of sunlight along the railing of his porch. He started to make pencil marks on the bannister, tracking the tree's height every few days, and he marveled at how something he watched so closely could still change and grow without him even noticing.

Some days, his neighbor would wave as he drove to and from work. Some days, he'd let out a sharp little beep from his tiny car. Some days, Harold would even wave back.

* * *

By summer, Harold started to wonder what type of peach he'd planted. He doubted it had been labeled at the grocery store, and even if it had been, he didn't remember now. He pulled down the rickety steps to his attic, where he knew her books were. She'd planted a small garden, had it for years before she'd gone. That's how he thought of her, even now. Gone. It was easier that way at first, less final. She could come back from being gone. She'd gone to the store, and then come back. She'd gone for a walk, and then come back. She'd gone to the hospital, and here he was, still waiting for her to come back.

He'd eventually thrown down grass seed to fill in her garden, but by then the weeds had taken over, and it was years and years before the long rectangle completely blended in with the rest of the yard. When the light hit the plot right, in the late afternoon when the sun was low in the west, he could still see the shadowed edges of it. Long ago he'd tried to find the feel of those edges, walking the shadows, running his foot along the dark lines, but though he could remember and even still see that part of his past, he could no longer feel it.

He dug through the boxes—through old romance novels and cookbooks, stories of families and the great and terrible things that happened to them, a faded copy of *The Joy of Sex* he didn't remember her having—and finally found her gardening encyclopedia. Inside were scraps of paper, notes in her handwriting of planting dates and harvest numbers, and then he finally got to the Ps, to peaches and their varietals. He skimmed through the names and pictures—August Pride and Babcock and Cardinal and so on—and though there were some obvious differences, his tree was too young to identify. It just looked like a little tree. Still, he ran his finger down the page and imagined the friction of his skin on the paper releasing the scent of peaches. Coronet and Cresthaven and Desert Gold. Garnet Beauty and Gold Dust. Harken and Harmony. He laughed at Honey Babe. *Is that what I should call you? Honey Babe?*

He traced his finger down the page and on to the next, but he wasn't reading anymore. It was ridiculous, but he knew he was stuck with it now. *Honey Babe.* He was smiling, alone in the heat of the attic, when the doorbell rang. He shuffled to the wall and peeked out the gable vent, but he couldn't see anyone. Didn't even see a car. He thought about Honey Babe out on the porch. No one would steal a little tree, he was certain, but still he felt a thin ripple of fear. He dropped the book back in the box and climbed carefully down the stairs.

By the time he got to the door, the person was walking back down the driveway. Honey Babe was still in her spot. The man in the driveway had dark hair, a plaid shirt; dressed nice. Probably selling something. He cut across Harold's grass, toward the line of fir trees separating his yard from the neighbor's house, and then he recognized the profile. His neighbor, the one who waved from the car. Harold opened the door.

"What'd you want?" he yelled.

The man stopped and waved, jogged back with a smile. "Hi! Hello!" He stopped at the bottom of the porch stairs. "I live next door. Mike." He took the first step and held out a hand. The man's weight on the stairs made Honey Babe wobble on the rail, and Harold put a hand out to steady her. Harold frowned down at the man's feet, but he didn't seem to notice.

"We've been waving for a while, figured I should finally get around to introducing myself."

"Harold," he said, shaking his hand, steadying Honey Babe with the other.

"You lived here long?"

"You could say that."

"We moved in last year. But you probably knew that already."

Harold had no idea. Wasn't even sure who lived there before this guy. The goings-on past the property line never interested him much. Except that one asshole years ago who'd cut his grass every Saturday morning at dawn. So goddamn impressed by his riding mower. He wasn't sorry when that one keeled over. But after him Harold never had much cause to pay attention to anyone past the tree line.

"Anyway, we're having a little cookout this weekend. Memorial Day and all. We wanted to invite you over. It'll start around one, only a few people. If you'd like."

"Oh." Harold gripped Honey Babe's pot tighter. He looked from the plant to Mike. "No, that's all right."

"It's no trouble. You'd be more than welcome."

"No. Thank you, though."

Mike stood at the bottom of the step, looking up at Harold, who looked at Honey Babe. "Well, if you change your mind," Mike said. "You know where we live."

"Right there," Harold said, pointing. He flushed. A dumb thing to say.

Mike laughed. "Yep, right there." He finally took a foot off the step. "It was nice meeting you. Feel free to stop by if you change your mind."

Harold watched him walk away, the man occasionally glancing back over his shoulder, giving Harold one last wave as he disappeared through the trees.

He came again with another invitation on the Fourth of July. Again in August for no real reason. And then again before Labor Day when Harold had had enough and finally gave in. He'd show up once and they'd get over their sense of obligation and then get back to leaving him alone.

By then, Honey Babe had grown tall enough Harold had to put her in a new pot, a dark blue glaze with a red terracotta rim. He'd shown the lady in the garden section a picture of her, asked what size pot was best, and if she knew what varietal she might be. The lady squinted and said, "Hard to say. You'll have to wait till she fruits in a year or two."

I might be dead by then, Harold thought. She probably wouldn't have known anyway. Last time he was there she worked in the plumbing section.

He checked the weather, warm and clear, and decided to leave her on the porch. "I'll be right over there," he said. Honey Babe stood there in her pot. He shook his head, laughed at himself. Going crazy in his old age.

"Next thing you know I'll be hiring a babysitter to watch my tree." But at the property line he felt a pang, hard and sharp enough that he stopped. He looked back at the house, at the tree sitting in the sun in front of the porch. He looked down his driveway. No one would bother her. No one ever came around. But deer? Did deer eat peach trees? No, he didn't think so. Right? He almost turned back, ready to climb up into the attic and pull down the old gardening book to find out what might hurt her, find out everything he needed to do to protect her.

A rush of something like shame hit him them. Not quite shame, but something close to it he couldn't quite name. "It's only a tree," he said, and pushed through into his neighbor's yard.

The smell of meat searing on the grill wafted around him, the rich scent of charcoal and charred fat. Music drifted out of the house. A few people sat around in chairs on a stone patio, laughing and smiling at each other, sipping from beer bottles. There were a couple of kids bouncing on a trampoline in the far reaches of the yard. He stopped and watched them. He didn't know kids lived here.

"Harold! You came!"

"Yeah, well." Harold shrugged. "You kept asking."

Mike laughed. "I did. Let me introduce you."

Harold drowned in a sea of new faces, names forgotten the moment he let go of their hands, though he tried. The lady was a doctor, he could remember that. And the guy in the pink shorts was name Brian or Byron. Something with a B. He sat amiably, quietly drinking the beer he was handed. They seemed interested to hear about the history of their sparse little neighborhood: the farmland it used to be, the ice storm and how they were stranded without power for two weeks, the stream that used to run through the woods, before the loggers came and it silted up from all the runoff.

Harold had to admit it was nice, sitting with other people, talking and listening to them talk, hearing voices from something other than the TV. The beer warmed him even as the night started to cool. Even as people drifted away, Harold stayed. Eventually, only Mike and another man remained. He had been introduced but now, with the beer and the rush of all these new faces and getting so damned old, he couldn't remember his name.

"You guys brothers?" Harold said. "You look alike."

Mike laughed. "That's Seth, remember?"

"Sorry. So many new people."

"He's my husband."

"Oh." Harold looked at the boy and girl bouncing on the trampoline. "But how'd you get them?"

Mike laughed. "Bought' em."

"Mike," Seth said, shaking his head at Harold.

"Well, we did. Technically."

"We *adopted* them. We didn't *buy* them."

"What's left of my bank account says we bought them. But yes, we also adopted them. Adopted them and poverty."

"You have any kids, Harold?" Seth asked.

Almost, Harold thought, but he just shook his head.

Mike and Seth looked at each other.

"I could never afford any," Harold said.

The three laughed. Seth excused himself and went to jump on the trampoline with the kids. Harold wasn't sure how old they were, but they both looked little. Maybe six or seven? Hard to say so far away.

"Allie and Nick." Mike pointed to the bouncing kids.

Harold nodded, but inside he was pushing the names away, burying them next to other names long unsaid. "Were they siblings, you know, before?"

Mike nodded. "Twins. Two-for-one deal." Mike smiled.

"Seth hates that joke, too."

"What's it like, being married to a man?" Harold wasn't sure where all these questions were coming from, but he was glad Mike didn't seem annoyed.

Mike thought about Harold's question for a moment. "Were you ever married?"

"A long time ago. To a woman."

"I figured." Mike smiled and sipped his beer. "Well, other than the fact we can share clothes, it's probably not too much different, I think. Agreements and disagreements. Fights and making up. Good and bad. Light and dark, like any married couple. You work to stay in the light as best you can."

Harold nodded, looking down at his hands, then over at the kids popping high in the air every time Seth came down hard on the trampoline, bouncing them into the surrounding net before they collapsed to the mat, laughing. He thought of his wife, the way she used to wear his flannel shirts out gardening.

A lightbulb flicked on, flooding the patio. Must have been some sort of sensor. It had grown quite dark. Out in the falling night Harold could still hear the children bouncing and laughing but he could no longer see them. The line of trees separating the houses had blurred into a tall, black wall.

"I should head back," Harold said, setting down his empty bottle. "Get Honey Babe in."

"Who?"

Harold froze and stammered. "I just, I should get back."

"Honey Babe your cat or something?"

"Yeah," Harold said. "A cat. An old cat." Harold nodded off toward the children and Seth. "Tell them I said goodbye, and thank you for having me."

"We should do this again. You gonna be okay getting home?"

Harold nodded and walked carefully into the dark. "I'll be fine. I know the way."

* * *

The fall was warm, and Harold spent much of it puttering around his yard with Honey Babe perched in the sun, looking on. He'd neglected the yard for years, barely noticing as crabgrass and bare patches spread, the old flowerbed by the driveway choked with weeds. He decided it was time to fix it up, the front yard at least. Give him something to do.

He scraped up the dead patches and spread grass seed and fertilizer, watched the thin green haze spread around the flower bed and over the bare dirt.

He planted some tulip bulbs, orange and purple and pink and red, a riot of future color. He spread a few bags of dark brown mulch, carefully tending the edges. Mike had seen him unloading the bags from the bed of the old pickup truck and helped him dump them around the flower bed. The children had come with him, happy to play in the dirt. Harold had a few bulbs left, and he let them plant them. He'd steered them away from the center of the bed but didn't tell them why. Every few days they came over and checked on their flowers, no matter how many times he told them they wouldn't bloom until spring. But a few days is a season for a small child, and so he got used to looking out the window and seeing them in his yard, inspecting the empty flower bed before scurrying back to their house.

After every improvement to the yard, he would ask Honey Babe what she thought. It would be her new home, though he tried to push the thought aside as best he could. He knew he needed to plant her before the ground froze. He'd checked the records in an old almanac, then called the county extension office for their advice. Both the book and the lady at the extension office said no later than the first of November. But even that seemed too soon. He wished he could get to Thanksgiving with her. Perhaps the fall had been warm enough to grant them a few extra weeks, but he knew he shouldn't risk it.

At Halloween, Mike and Seth brought the kids over. The little boy was dressed as a zombie, the girl as Princess Leia. Harold felt a moment of panic when he saw them through the thin curtain covering his front window. "Hang on a minute," he yelled. He scrambled through the kitchen cabinets for candy, coming up with nothing but dusty cans of fruit.

The kids were murmuring behind the door, and Harold resigned himself to disappointing them. As he opened the door, the words "I'm sorry" leaping out ahead of him, Mike stepped forward into the doorway and said "Hey, Harold!" pretending to shake his hand but instead pressing two small bags of candy into his palm. Then he stepped away, leaving Harold holding the candy right in front of the children's faces, their eyes exploding with delight. It was almost a magic trick.

They talked for a few moments, the children telling him about their costumes and all the candy they were going to get. As Seth and the kids walked back toward their house, Mike stayed.

"I haven't gotten trick-or-treaters in years," Harold said.

"I figured. A bit too spread out here for many. We're going to drive them into town, go on some of the side streets."

"Sounds like fun."

"You want to come? We'll be done by dark. Seth's got a night shift at the hospital starting in a few hours anyway."

"Oh, no. Too old for all that."

"Oh, come on. Put some gas in your walker and let's go."

"I don't use a walker," Harold said, indignant.

"It was a joke. Come on, it'll be fun."

Harold looked past Mike, at the kids tottering away into the dark. He looked at Honey Babe, her heavy pot tucked next to the door. He had planned to get the hole ready this afternoon so he could get her in the ground tomorrow.

"What, you got plans? Come on, the kids will love it."

"Well, all right." Harold pulled his coat from the hook by the door. In his head, he told Honey Babe he would be back soon, then stepped outside.

Trick or treating was a whirlwind of squeals and hordes of little monsters, overwhelming in its way. The kids bounced from one door to the next, came running back waving shiny little candy bars, plastic vampire fangs, stickers, foil-wrapped chocolates.

"You guys are making out like bandits!" Harold said.

At one house, they pulled him to the front door with them.

"And what are you supposed to be?" the lady who answered the door asked him.

Harold looked down at his faded flannel shirt and corduroy pants and thick-soled sneakers. "An old man, I guess."

She laughed. "Must be one of the good ones then, if you've got grandkids as sweet as these," and before he could correct her, she gave him his own little bag of candy, which he tucked into his shirt pocket.

"Looks like the kids aren't the only ones making out like bandits, Harry," Mike said. "You get her number?"

"Oh hush," Harold said, his face burning red.

Eventually, the kids grew tired and cold, and Seth had to go to work, so they packed everyone up and drove back home. They dropped Harold off at his front porch, and he stood and waved as they backed down the driveway. He shivered a bit at the chill in the air. The moon rose over the trees as the light faded. Leaves rustled as they blew across the lawn and fell from the trees, blanketing the yard in oranges and reds. They seemed to be falling faster, he thought, as if time, already so short, was speeding up here at the end of the season.

As he sat in his recliner eating his candy that night, he thought of Mike calling him Harry. No one had ever called him that. Not his parents, not his friends when he was a kid. Not even his wife. He began to toy with the name in his head. *Harry. Harry. Harry and Honey Babe. Harry and his friend Mike. Harry, the old man trick-or-treating. Harry, eating candy and watching the weather report.*

It was watching the weather that eventually broke him away from this small contentment. A storm was coming, they said. In two days, there might be a foot of snow. He hung on the words, parsing each little bit of doubt in the phrasing. *Early in the season to be too confident. Could veer off. Percentages. Chances.*

He had to get her in the ground tomorrow then. He should have done it today, dammit. Now it had to be done tomorrow. She was ready, even if he wasn't. Her leaves had grown pale and stiff. They crinkled when he touched them, falling to rest at the base of her trunk or tumbling down to the scuffed wood floor.

* * *

The next afternoon, he took her out to the front flower bed. He'd readied everything: his shovel and trowel, a small bag of compost, fresh mulch. He scraped away the layer of old mulch and leaves, and then pressed the spade into the soil. The edge sliced an inch into the soil, then stopped. He pressed his foot against it, and it slipped slightly deeper. He leaned into as best he could without losing his balance, and it barely budged. The sky above was slate gray and the air bit into the sheen of sweat on his skin. He kept digging, slowly making the hole wider and deeper. At times it was less like digging and more like shaving away the hardened dirt. He dragged over the hose, filling it with water, hoping to soften it. It worked a bit, and he made faster progress, but he was exhausted and dizzy by the time the hole was large enough.

He pulled Honey Babe near and tilted her gently on her side, carefully running his trowel along the inside edge to loosen her grip on the pot. As he eased her out, the roots tore away from the glazed pot with a sound that reminded him of Velcro. It echoed in his head, thumping against his skull at the same rhythm as his heart pounding in his chest. He slipped her out and onto the ground and took a deep breath, her roots ghostly white and densely woven through the black dirt, practically rootbound. He pulled her closer to the hole, gently loosening her roots so she could catch hold of her new home.

The air blasted through his thin shirt, the leaden sky pressed down on him, and he worried again he'd waited too long. He tried to catch his breath and the cold burned his throat. A few drops of rain splashed down, leaving dark spots on his sleeves. They doubled, multiplied, his arm growing full of dark spots, and he realized it wasn't rain but his vision. He felt the pressure in his chest, the electric shocks racing up his side, and then he knew. Through the trees, Mike's house was a dark mass, no light in the windows, no car in the driveway.

He pushed himself up on one knee but could not steady himself to get to his feet. The walk to the house, the front steps, the door, they all seemed like impossible obstacles. *Another dead old man frozen to his shovel,* he thought, and he would have laughed a little if the lightning striking inside his chest had let up for even a moment.

* * *

The cold saved him, or played a part anyway. That, and Mike and Seth driving home at the right time. That's what the nurse told him when he finally woke in the hospital. Told him about the heart attack, the cold slowing the damage, Seth and the CPR and the ambulance. They'd taken good care of him, the two had been to visit, he'd spoken to them but probably didn't remember.

The nurse smiled when he asked about the weather. The storm had come after all, earlier than expected, she said, and worse than they'd thought. She opened the blinds so he could see how white the world was still. She set a box of tissues on his lap, told him it was fine, this was normal when you've been through so much, it was okay to let it all out.

* * *

A few hours later, Seth and Mike walked in. Seth wore scrubs and Mike had a bright green visitor sticker on his shirt. "I heard you were awake," Seth said. "I called Mike right away."

Mike sat down, asked the usual hospital bedside questions. Harold nodded a response to some of them, but others he just looked away.

Seth and Mike gave each other a look, then Seth squeezed Mike's arm and stepped out.

"Listen. I don't think you remember, but you kept going on and on, asking me to find your cat before the storm came. To get her inside. I swear I looked everywhere, Harry, but I couldn't find her."

Harold shook his head. "My cat?"

"Honey Babe," Mike said. "I looked everywhere. Called her for hours. I went back the next day, too. I looked inside and out but there wasn't any cat." Mike took a deep breath. "I've been going over every day, but I still haven't been able to find her. I—" He paused and put his hand on Harold's. "Harry, I can't even find any clue you ever had a cat. No food. No litter box. Nothing."

Harold turned and pulled his hand away. "It doesn't matter. She's gone."

* * *

Eventually, Harold was allowed home. But the snow never seemed to clear that winter. He knew out there, beneath it all, Honey Babe lay with her tender roots encased in ice.

Christmas came and went. Mike and Seth would check on him, but Harold wouldn't open the door. He'd yell that he was fine, tell them not to worry, eventually tell them to outright go away and leave him alone. They would wait at the door for a long time before giving up.

At Christmas, Mike and Seth and the kids tried to give him a present. They'd eventually grown cold and left it by the door. Later, when Harold finally brought it in and opened it, he found a framed picture of the five of them, the kids dressed in their Halloween costumes and holding bright orange plastic pumpkins.

"To Harry, who has the best Old Man costume" was written in silver ink in the corner.

He left it face down on the kitchen counter.

Every few days they would stop by, even though Harold never let them in. As time went on, the knocks became less insistent. The days between them longer. The time they waited for him to open up grew shorter.

"We're going to find him dead in there someday," he'd heard Seth say one day before turning and walking away. Mike waited a few moments longer before giving up, too.

* * *

Around Valentine's Day, Mike showed up again. He pounded on the door.

"I'm fine," Harold yelled.

"No, you're not." Mike's voice rippled with a foreign anger.

Harold walked to the door. Mike looked like a paler version of himself through the thin white curtain. He stood holding a big paper bag. "You think I don't know if I'm fine?" Harold said. "I'm telling you, I'm fine. Get out of here."

"Listen, I don't know why you're doing this. I'm sorry this happened. I'm sorry about Honey Babe. I tried, but maybe I should have tried harder." Mike looked down and shook his head.

Harold could feel the pain and anger and sadness all bubbling together inside him. *She wasn't a cat. She was a tree. She was mine and I was taking care of her and now she's dead, buried over there somewhere under the snow because I'm too damn old to do anything about it. I couldn't keep her alive and I couldn't protect her and now she's gone. Gone.*

Tears burned their way to the surface, and he palmed them away. He knew Mike could see him through the curtain and he turned his back.

"Come on, Harry." Mike's voice had softened. "Open the door."

Behind Harold, the doorknob rattled, but it was locked.

The two of them stood that way for a long while, Mike just outside and Harold turned away, his shoulders heaving and finally settling as his quiet sobs filtered through the locked door.

"I brought these for you," Mike finally said. The paper bag crinkled as he set it in front of the door. "We're right next door, right there, when you need us."

Mike's footsteps echoed off the porch and crunched out into the snow. When the footsteps faded, Harold finally turned back and looked. Mike was halfway across the yard when Harold opened the door, but he must not have heard it unlatch and creak open because he didn't stop or turn back to look. Harold watched him go.

He picked up the bag, bread and eggs balanced on a deep pile of groceries, and carried it inside. He shut the door, but this time didn't lock it.

He set the bag on the counter and pulled out the eggs and bread resting on top. He propped up the picture frame against the wall to make room for the rest, the orange pumpkins and the silver writing catching the light. The kids, Allie and Nick, smiling wide. Harold looked closer, and saw he was smiling, too. He pulled out the rest of the groceries. A small carton of milk. Some slices of cheese and deli meat. Coffee. Yogurt. Each item he set gently on the counter in front of the picture.

Finally, at the bottom, sat a small bag of peaches. He lifted them and they spun slowly as the twisted bag unwound, the plastic wrinkles straightening and disappearing. He set it on the counter and tore through the thin plastic membrane, the sweet scent of the fruit flooding his nose.

He picked up a peach, the skin dimpling under his fingers even though he held it carefully. He pressed until his thumb broke through and released a trickle of peach juice that dripped down his hand and ticked onto the counter. He sucked the juice from his pale wrist, then pressed the peach to his lips, like kissing the forehead of a newborn baby, or the curve of a woman's neck, the skin velvety and smooth and covered in ghostly golden hairs.

Harold bit into the peach and his mouth flooded with sweetness. He closed his eyes and ate until the flesh was gone and all that remained was the dark pit, resting in his palm like an old, shriveled heart, the sprig of life inside pulsing in its own slow, patient rhythm, waiting for him to find it again.

ACKNOWLEDGMENTS

"Coyotes," a 2017 winner of the Maine Literary Award for Short Fiction, was previously published by *The Forge Literary Magazine*, where it was nominated for a Pushcart Prize.

First, a thank you to my teachers and mentors. I am eternally grateful for the many ways your lessons continue to shape my writing and my life.

Thank you to Alan Heathcock, Rebecca Makkai, Mike McCormack, Steve Woodward, Alexi Zentner, Benjamin Percy, Christian Kiefer, Laura Wetherington, Lewis Robinson, and Pam Houston. I've been so incredibly lucky to learn this craft from each of you.

Thank you to Sally Shivnan, for laying the foundation. Thank you to Chris Corbett for teaching me the power and value of every precisely chosen word.

For "Coyotes," thank you again to Pam, Mike, and Lewis, who helped shepherd that story along during its long development, and helped shape it into something I could be proud of.

Thank you to Steve Almond, whose workshops helped give "Animal Sacrifices" a narrator with some heart. And thank you to Josh Bodwell for the support over the years, and for handing me the Andre Dubus collection *The Winter Father*, to which "Animal Sacrifices" owes a debt.

Thanks to Justin Torres, whose prompt (select an abstract concept, a man-made item, and an organic object, then cycle through all four seasons) in a virtual writing workshop during lockdown sparked "Honey Babe." And thanks to the other participants who chose the elements (regret, a shower head, a peach, and start in winter).

Thank you to the Maine Writers & Publishers Alliance for providing so many opportunities to learn, and for all the support over the years.

Thank you to Monson Arts and The Libra Foundation for the time and space to write.

Thank you to Brian Turner, June Sylvester Saraceno, and everyone at the Sierra Nevada University MFA program for preparing me for the path between two pines.

A special thank you to Ray Brunt, Kathleen Flear, Courtney Harler, and Kari Shemwell. Your friendship has made my life and my writing so much better.

Thank you to my parents, who rarely said no when I begged for books from the racks at the grocery store.

And finally, thank you to my family: Becky, Sam, and Liam. There are so many words, but none could ever fully express my love and gratitude. I couldn't do any of this without you. I love you.

ABOUT THE
MAINE WRITERS & PUBLISHERS ALLIANCE

Founded in 1975 by a group of small presses and writers, Maine Writers & Publishers Alliance (MWPA) has worked for decades to enrich the literary life and culture of Maine. We bring together Maine writers, editors, publishers, booksellers, and literary professionals at all stages of their careers to sharpen craft, create community, and celebrate great writing. MWPA has an active, growing membership of more than 1,400 literary professionals from all sixteen counties of the state. In 2020, the MWPA held sixty-four writing conferences and workshops in locations across Maine, as well as more than one hundred free readings and community events, moving all our programs online during the pandemic. To help make our memberships, conferences, and workshops accessible, MWPA offered more than $23,000 in scholarships to Maine writers at all stages of their careers last year.

ABOUT THE MAINE CHAPBOOK SERIES

Between 1983 and 1999, thirteen chapbooks were published by the Maine Arts Commission in collaboration with a series of small Maine presses, and then by the Maine Writers & Publishers Alliance, as part of the Maine Chapbook Series. Each year, a nationally known writer served as the judge and selected a manuscript for publication. In 2019, the MWPA re-started this beloved series.

PREVIOUS MAINE CHAPBOOK SERIES WINNERS

Ruth Mendelson, *Sixteen Pastorals*
Theodore Press, 1983
Selected by Philip Booth

Rebecca Cummings, *Kaisa Kilponen*
Coyote Love Press, 1986
Selected by George Garrett

Robert Chute, *Samuel Sails for Home*
Coyote Love Press, 1987
Selected by Charles Simic

Christopher Fahy,
One Day in the Short Happy Life of Anna Banana
Coastwise Press, 1988
Selected by Mary McCarthy

Kenneth Rosen, *The Hebrew Lion*
Ascensius Press, 1989
Selected by Amy Clampitt

Denis Ledoux, *Mountain Dance*
Coastwise Press, 1990
Selected by Elizabeth Hardwick

Besty Sholl, *Pick a Card*
Coyote/Bark Publications, 1991
Selected by Donald Hall

John A.S. Rogers, *The Elephant on the Tracks and Other Stories*
Muse Press, 1994
Selected by David Huddle

Candice Stover, *Holding Patterns*
Muse Press, 1994
Selected by Mary Oliver

Sis Deans, *Decisions and Other Stories*
Maine Writers & Publishers Alliance, 1995
Selected by Cathie Pelletier

Peter Harris, *Blue Hallelujahs*
Maine Writers & Publishers Alliance, 1996
Selected by Roland Flint

Rhea Cote Robbins, *Wednesday's Child*
Maine Writers & Publishers Alliance, 1997
Selected by Sven Birkerts

Ellen Bryan Obed, *A Letter from the Snow*
Maine Author's Publishing, 1999
Selected by Lois Lowry

Suzanne Langlois, *Bright Glint Gone*
Maine Writers & Publishers Alliance, 2019
Selected by Martha Collins

ABOUT THE AUTHOR

Brandon Dudley is a graduate of the MFA program at Sierra Nevada University, where he was managing editor of the *Sierra Nevada Review*. His short fiction has won a Maine Literary Award and he has been a Monson Arts fellow. His stories, essays, interviews, and criticism have appeared or are forthcoming in *New South, The Millions, The Forge, Fiction Writers Review,* and others. A former journalist, he now teaches high school English in Brunswick, Maine, where he lives with his wife and two sons.